It was the night before Christmas. Holly put a mince pie and a glass of lemonade on the table.

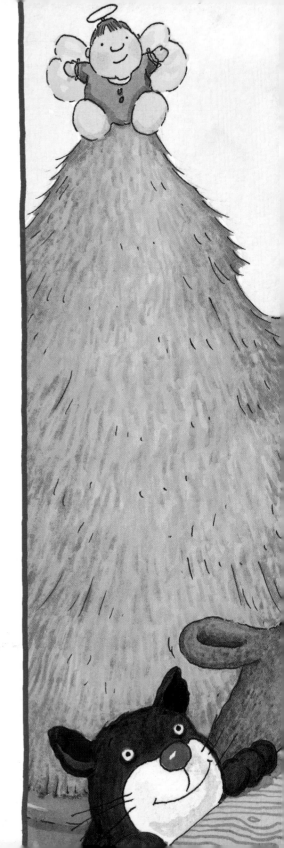

"I want to stay up and see Father Christmas," she said.

"He won't come until much later, when you're fast asleep in bed," said Dad as he carried her upstairs.

Holly hung her stocking at the end of the bed and Dad tucked her in.

"Goodnight, Holly!" he said. "The sooner you go to sleep, the sooner Father Christmas will come."

But Holly was too excited to sleep. She lay in bed, listening...

After a while she heard
a soft *tinkle, tinkle*.

"Is that you, Father
Christmas?" she
whispered.

But it was only the
church bells ringing
far away.

A little later she heard a *whoosh! whoosh!* just outside her window.

"Is that you, Father Christmas?" she whispered.

But it was only the wind, blowing through the trees.

Even later she heard
a *crackle! crackle!*

"Is that you, Father
Christmas?" she
whispered.

But it was
only Kitty pouncing
on the wrapping paper.

Soon after that she heard a *thud! thud!* at the bottom of the stairs.

"Is that you, Father Christmas?" she whispered.

But it was only Betsy, banging her tail on the floor.

Then she heard
a *creak! creak!* of
floorboards.

"Is that you, Father
Christmas?" she
whispered.

But it was only Mum
and Dad on their way
to bed.

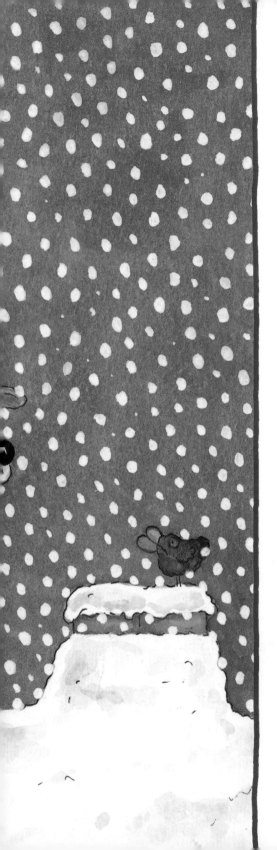

All of a sudden the air was filled with the *jingle jangle! jingle jangle!* of sleigh bells. The reindeer landed, *CRUNCH!* on the crispy, white snow.

Father Christmas tumbled down the chimney, *BUMP! BUMP! BUMP!*

And he went upstairs,
THUMP! THUMP! THUMP!

But Holly didn't hear
a sound …

she was
fast asleep
in bed.

Happy Christmas,
Holly!

For Lukas

JPIC
1309578

First published 2000 by Walker Books Ltd
87 Vauxhall Walk, London SE11 5HJ

This edition published 2002

2 4 6 8 10 9 7 5 3 1

© 2000 Siobhan Dodds

The right of Siobhan Dodds to be identified as author of this work has been asserted
by her in accordance with the Copyright, Designs and Patents Act 1988

This book has been typeset in Usherwood

Printed in Hong Kong

British Library Cataloguing in Publication Data:
a catalogue record for this book is available from the British Library

ISBN 0-7445-9428-6